PONDERS

Enter the world of "the ponders", the creatures who live in or around the country pond, in these eight, highly original stories.

Born in Lansdale, Pennsylvania, Russell Hoban was an illustrator before he became a writer. Among his books for adults is the modern classic *Riddley Walker*. He has written more than sixty picture books for children, including *The Sea-thing Child*, as well as two books of poetry and the novel *The Mouse and His Child*. He lives in London.

Withdrawn Stock
Cavan County Library

*Charlie Meadows's little black shadow began to dance
and he had to dance and change his shape with it.*

Ponders

Written by
RUSSELL HOBAN

Illustrated by
MARTIN BAYNTON

WALKER BOOKS
AND SUBSIDIARIES
LONDON • BOSTON • SYDNEY

To the memory of Ferd Monjo

CAVAN COUNTY LIBRARY

ACC. No. C.1127.38.....

CLASS No. ..J..............

INVOICE NO. 4778..1ES.

PRICE £4..16./E5.28

/ / JAN 2003

First published 1988 by
Walker Books Ltd, 87 Vauxhall Walk
London SE11 5HJ

This edition published 1999

2 4 6 8 10 9 7 5 3 1

Text © 1983, 1984, 1988 Russell Hoban
Illustrations © 1988 Martin Baynton

Printed in England by Clays Ltd, St Ives plc

British Library Cataloguing in Publication Data
A catalogue record for this book is available
from the British Library.

ISBN 0-7445-7226-6

CONTENTS

"Nobody likes me," said Jim.
"Everybody hates me."

JIM
FROG

Jim Frog was feeling a little low, a little lonely, he had no hop in him, he just dragged himself along.

At chorus practice he wouldn't sit up straight on his lily pad, he just flopped around. When everyone else croaked "Jug-of-rum" he croaked "Mug-of-jum".

"Stop that!" everyone shouted. "Why can't you croak 'Jug-of-rum' like the rest of us?"

"Nobody likes me," said Jim. "Everybody hates me."

When it was snack time everybody else got their nets and went out to catch dragonflies. Jim couldn't be bothered, he wasn't hungry, he couldn't find his net, he didn't care. He took his harmonica out of his pocket and played sad songs.

A head came out of the water, it was Big John Turkle the snapper.

When Jim saw Big John he hopped away fast.

"Nobody likes me," said Big John Turkle. "Everybody hates me."

Jim swam down to the other end of the pond. He stuck his head up through the duckweed and saw a damselfly nymph crawling slowly up a cat-tail stem.

"Go ahead," said the nymph. "Eat me, I don't care."

"I'm not hungry," said Jim.

"Everything's been so utterly rotten," said the nymph.

"I've been feeling low too," said Jim.

"Everything seems to be closing in on

me," said the nymph. "I can scarcely breathe, I feel as if I'm going to jump out of my skin."

"I feel a little lonely," said Jim.

He was looking away from the damselfly nymph when he said that. When he looked back there was her empty skin split down the back and the damselfly was out of it.

She looked altogether different, she waved her new wings dry, then she flew away blue and glittering across the pond.

"How did she do that?" said Jim. "I wonder if I can do it." He climbed onto a lily pad and tried to jump out of his skin but his skin jumped with him.

"Ladies and gentlemen," said a voice, "your attention, please: Roland Waters the pond-famous diving beetle will now dive from a height of one inch into two feet of water."

The voice belonged to Roland himself. "Drum roll, please," he said to the cicada who was his partner.

The cicada did the drum roll and Roland dived into the water.

"Did you see that?" he said to Jim. "What a feat!"

"I thought it was two feet," said Jim.

"What a joker you are," said Roland. "But it really was something, wasn't it? I think everyone was impressed."

Jim looked all around but he couldn't see anyone but the cicada, who was dozing in the sun.

"I suppose they were," said Jim.

He felt like being alone so he went down to the bottom of the pond and swam into a hollow log. He took his harmonica out of his pocket and began to play it.

Big John Turkle looked in. The hole in

the log was too narrow for him so Jim was safe there.

"I can see the bubbles but I can't hear any music," said Big John.

"Neither can I," said Jim, "but I know what I'm playing."

"Is it happy or sad?" said Big John.

"Sad," said Jim.

"That's funny," said Big John, "the bubbles look happy."

Jim went home. He noticed that he had a lot of hop in him. He thought of Roland Waters and he began to laugh. He was laughing and hopping, laughing and hopping all the way home.

When he got home his mother said, "You look as if you've been having a pretty good day."

"Actually it hasn't been bad," said Jim, "not bad at all."

*Nothing was going right for Big John Turkle.
He'd almost caught a duck but it got away.*

BIG JOHN
TURKLE

Big John Turkle was not having a good day. Nothing was going right for him. He'd almost caught a duck but it got away.

Big John swam down to his sulking place. There he grumbled and cursed and sang his bother song:

"Bother here and bother there,
Too much bother everywhere."

Big John began to think of lobster salad. He had had some only once, part of a sandwich dropped into the pond by a picnicker in a rowboat. He thought of how it would be to have a whole plate of lobster-salad sandwiches to himself.

He swam up to the surface, then he swam slowly up and down the pond with just his head sticking up out of the water like a periscope.

The boat was hauled up on the bank and there were no picnickers to be seen anywhere. The sky was grey, the wind was riffling the water.

There were mallards on the pond, some of them were up-ending while others bobbed

like boats at anchor.

Big John thought he heard them laughing as he swam past.

He climbed onto a log that leant up against the bank. He listened to the wind rattling the brown oak leaves.

Big John looked up and saw Grover Crow flying backwards. He would fly up into the wind and let it blow him back a little way, then he would flap and flutter down to the ground and hop around chuckling to himself before he flew up again.

"What are you laughing about?" said Big John.

Grover Crow cocked his head to one side and looked at Big John.

"I've got a willow-pattern cup handle," he said, "and quite a bit of the cup as well. How about that?"

"Have you got any lobster salad?" said Big John.

"Lobster salad is not an object of art," said Grover Crow.

"Object of art!" said Big John. "You don't know what life's all about!"

"Don't I!" said Grover Crow. "Have *you* got a willow-pattern cup handle?"

"Flobbery!" said Big John. "That's just a lot of flummery old flobbery."

"You say that because you can't think of

anything else to say," said Grover Crow, "and because you haven't got a willow-pattern cup handle."

Big John slid into the water without a word, leaving a stream of angry bubbles behind him as he swam to the bottom. He tried to remember how the lobster salad had tasted but the taste would not come back to him.

He swam up to the surface again and saw Grover Crow swaggering around with the willow-pattern cup handle in his beak and crooning to himself. Grover did not see Big John. When he had finished parading with his art object he carefully hid it under some dead leaves. Then he flew off, laughing to himself.

"Flibbery," said Big John.

As soon as Grover Crow was out of sight Big John hustled over to where the cup

Big John closed his eyes and with a smile on his face he went to sleep for the winter.

handle was hidden, uncovered it, and took it back to the pond with him.

Just before he slid into the water he looked up at the grey sky. The sky was looking wintry, it made him feel sleepy.

Big John swam down to his winter bedroom under the mud. It was a cosy place with an oriental carpet and a four-poster bed. He put on his nightgown and nightcap, then he put the willow-pattern cup handle on the bedside table. Big John set his alarm clock for spring and crept under the covers.

"Ahhhh!" he sighed. He looked at the willow-pattern cup handle. "Well," he said, "it isn't lobster salad but at least Grover Crow hasn't got it."

Then he closed his eyes and with a smile on his face he went to sleep for the winter.

Charlie's paper was an old and yellowed torn-off scrap of headline. Charlie carried it in a cleft stick.

CHARLIE
MEADOWS

Charlie Meadows had a paper round. His paper was an old and yellowed torn-off scrap of headline. BLEAK OUTLO, it said. Charlie carried it in a cleft stick. When the other meadow mice saw the paper coming they knew that it was Charlie with the news and weather.

Charlie got the weather from his grandmother, she had rheumatism and she always knew when it was going to rain. The news he picked up as he made his round. Charlie always made his round between midnight and three o'clock in the morning. Every time he went out his mother said to him, "Look out for Ephraim Owl or *you'll* be in the news, Charlie Meadows."

Charlie always said he would be careful but he was perhaps not quite so careful as he might have been, he was too fond of moonlight. He especially liked the full-moon nights in winter when the shadows were black on the snow and the frozen pond creaked and his whiskers were stiff with the cold. Sometimes he would skate on the pond and on the frozen stream that ran through the meadow and the wood.

One full-moon night Ephraim Owl was sitting in a tall pine that overlooked the pond. There had just been a fresh snowfall and the ice on the pond was white under the moon.

Ephraim ruffled up his feathers and made himself bigger. "WHOOHOOHOO!" he hooted, and looked all round to see if anyone jumped up and ran.

"WHOOHOOHOOHOO!" he hooted again. Such a sudden sound, so strange! Even Ephraim wasn't sure if he had made it or if it had leapt out of the night all by itself.

When Charlie heard the hooting he was in the shadow of the pines on his way from Poverty Hollow to Frogtown Stump. Up he jumped and ran out into the whiteness of the frozen pond. His little black shadow began to dance, it kept changing its shape and Charlie had to dance and change his shape with it. The shadow of his cleft stick and paper grew long, grew short, spun round and round as he danced.

Down swooped Ephraim from the tall pine, down he swooped on silent wings with outstretched talons. Just as he was going to grab Charlie he drew back his talons and flew up again. He wanted Charlie for his supper but he didn't want Charlie's little shadow to stop dancing. He liked the way it whirled and changed its shape, he flew low over the ice and tried to make his shadow do the same, it seemed the proper thing to do with the moonlight.

Round and round went Charlie's shadow and Charlie, round and round went Ephraim's shadow and Ephraim. Ephraim's shadow got all mixed up with Charlie's shadow and Ephraim became confused.

He sat down suddenly on the ice while everything went round and round him. That was when Charlie noticed Ephraim for the first time. He too became confused, he stopped dancing and stood absolutely still, trembling all over and staring at Ephraim.

Ephraim looked at Charlie's paper. "What's that?" he said.

"BLEAK OUTLO," said Charlie.

"What's a BLEAK OUTLO?" said Ephraim.

*Ephraim sat down suddenly on the ice while
everything went round and round him.*

"It's a paper," said Charlie.

"I can see that it's a paper," said Ephraim. "But what does BLEAK OUTLO mean?"

"I don't know," said Charlie. "That's what it says on the paper."

"How do you know that's what it says?" said Ephraim.

"My grandmother told me," said Charlie.

"Oh," said Ephraim.

Ephraim began to think of supper again. He stood up and ruffled up all his feathers and made himself big. He spread his wings and leant low towards Charlie to show his ruffled-up back feathers and the tops of his wings so that Charlie could see how big he was. He snapped his bill and his yellow eyes stared straight at Charlie.

Charlie couldn't move, he stood there as if he were frozen to the spot, his little black shadow was perfectly motionless.

Ephraim looked at Charlie's shadow. "Oh, well," he said, "never mind." He made himself regular-size again. "You watch it next time," he said, and off he flew.

Charlie hurried on to Frogtown Stump. "BLEAK OUTLO news and weather," he said, "warm spell coming, rain and fog."

"What about the news?" said the Frogtown Stump mice.

"Ephraim Owl's out hunting by the pond," said Charlie.

"That's not news," said the Frogtown Stumpers.

"No," said Charlie, "I guess it isn't."

He never told what happened at the pond, he let that stay between him and Ephraim.

Lavinia's winter dreams were always pleasant,
always slow, never hurried.

LAVINIA
BAT

Hanging head down in her winter sleep Lavinia Bat was quite comfortable. Her winter dreams were always pleasant, always slow, never hurried.

In her dream the night was a lantern-globe of sound, it was lit with the colour of the wind, the rolling of the earth, the star-fires of crickets. It made a gentle hissing as it turned in space and all its skies turned with it.

Lavinia woke up, still half in her dream. She washed herself and stretched her wings and did her waking-up exercises. She flew up and down her cave, she did loops and turns, she did rolls and dives and figure eights. Then she went back to sleep.

In her dream Lavinia heard a whispering, she listened to it carefully.

"Pass it on," said the whispering.

"Pass what on?" said Lavinia.

"The something from the other," said the whispering.

"What other?" said Lavinia.

"The other dream," said the whispering.

Nights and days passed, the moon grew fat, grew thin, grew fat, grew thin. The skunk cabbages pushed up green points out of the ground, then the Jack-in-the-pulpits stood up in the boggy places and Big John Turkle climbed onto a log and tried out the sunlight.

Lavinia woke up. All she could remember was "Pass it on". But she couldn't remember what the something was that she was meant to pass on.

It was evening, it was spring, it was time to get moving. Outside the cave everything smelled wet and muddy and new.

What a singing there was at the pond! Jugs-of-rum were sung by the bullfrogs while others claimed that the water was only knee-deep, knee-deep. The peepers peeped constantly but they never told what they saw. "We peep, we peep!" was all they would say. Some of the insects said that Katy did, some said that Katy didn't, no one knew for sure.

Lavinia put her FM echolocator on SCAN, she put her computer on AUTOMATIC and she was ready to go. Other bats were coming out as well, all frequency bands were clicking and buzzing as they scrambled skitter-scattering, cornering into the night, they hadn't eaten since autumn.

What a skirmish for supper! The darkness

was full of buzzing, whirring and flapping things to eat. "CLICK CLICK CLICK CLICK CLICK," went Lavinia's scanner as it made its sweep, "BZZZZZZZZZZ!" as she zeroed in on her prey. Fat moths looped and turned and rolled and dived and Lavinia looped and turned and rolled and dived with them, some she caught and some she missed.

"JUG-OF-RUM!" sang Jim Frog and his crowd.

"Knee-deep!" sang the others.

"We peep!" sang the peepers.

"Katy did!" sang the katydids.

"Katy didn't!" sang the katydidn'ts.

"WHOOHOOHOO!" hooted Ephraim Owl.

"BLEAK OUTLO news and weather!" whispered Charlie Meadows.

"MOTH AT SIX O'CLOCK!" said Lavinia's scanner. "FOUR METRES AND CLOSING, THREE METRES, TWO..."

"DIVE!" said Lavinia's computer.

"I TASTE AWFUL!" ultrasounded the moth.

"Ptui!" said Lavinia, zooming up out of her dive and zeroing in on another moth.

"I TASTE AWFUL TOO!" ultrasounded that one.

"No, you don't," said Lavinia.

SCHLOOP!

What a supper that was, the first night of the spring outcoming!

Lavinia was listening to the night all round her and she was listening inside herself as well. She was going to have a baby.

"Ah!" said Lavinia, clicking to herself. She half remembered something but she half forgot it at the same time.

When Lavinia's time came her baby was born, it was a daughter and Lavinia named her Lola.

Lola was clever, she wanted to know

about everything. She said to Lavinia,
"How do you do bat work?"

Lavinia said, "Hang on and I'll show
you."

Lola hung on and Lavinia showed her.

"The main thing," said Lavinia, "is to get
tuned in."

"Tuned in to what?" said Lola.

"Everything," said Lavinia. She took Lola hunting with her and Lola got tuned in. She got tuned in to the night, she got tuned in to moving with it. Soon Lola was ready to hunt for herself. Off she went, cornering into the night.

Lavinia remembered her dreams then, remembered the lantern-globe of night, the hissing of it as it turned in space. Lavinia remembered the whispering that had said, "Pass it on!"

"Ah!" said Lavinia, clicking and buzzing, sweeping the night with her scanner and rolling with the rolling world.

"Ah!" said Lavinia, tuned into everything. "I've done that!"

*"Wow!" said Grover. "A shortwave radio.
I've heard about these."*

GROVER
CROW

Grover Crow was sorting through a few things at the dump when he happened on a combination lock. "Wow!" said Grover. "A shortwave radio. I've heard about these."

He turned the knob and listened to the clicks. "Listen to that!" he said. "Modern technology! That broadcast could be coming from outer space!"

"Don't be stupid," said his cousin Woodrow. "That's not a broadcast you're getting, this thing hasn't even got a battery in it." He pointed to the hole into which the shackle fitted when the lock was closed.

"You're the one that's stupid," said Grover. "That hole's for this other thing to fit into, probably that's how you turn it on. You hold it and I'll push."

Woodrow held while Grover pushed. After Grover had pushed Woodrow ten or fifteen feet without being able to close the lock he said, "This wants thinking on. Let's take it someplace where nobody'll bother us."

Grover took hold of the shackle with his beak and tried to take off. All of him took off except his head.

"I think it's too heavy," said Woodrow.

"I was just getting the feel of it," said Grover. "This is a two-crow job." He found a piece of twine. "Look," he said to Woodrow, "you take one end of the string in your beak and I'll take the other end in my beak and we'll hang the radio in the middle."

"How do we find the middle?" said Woodrow.

"Let's not talk about it," said Grover, "let's just do it." He ran the twine through the shackle, they each took one end of the twine, and off they flew with the lock swinging between them.

As they were flying over the pond Woodrow said, "I can't get over how you found the middle of the string." When he opened his beak to speak he let go of the string and the lock dropped like a bomb on the head of Big John Turkle, who was just coming up to the surface for a look round. Everything went black for Big John.

When he came to he said, "What kind of a tree did I swim under?" He stuck his head out of the water again and saw Grover and Woodrow standing on the bank.

"What happened?" he said.

"You were hit by a falling radio," said Grover.

"There," said Grover to Woodrow. "Now it's turned on and we ought to get something."

"What's a radio and who dropped it?" said Big John.

"Never mind," said Grover, "you can listen to lady turtles thousands of miles away singing songs if we can find it."

"This I've got to see," said Big John. He went down to the bottom of the pond and looked round until he found the lock. It had closed when it hit him on the head.

"There," said Grover to Woodrow. "Now it's turned on and we ought to get something." He turned the knob this way and that.

"What do you think you'll get turning that knob?" said Big John.

"Music and voices from far away," said Grover.

"You must be out of your mind," said Big John. "All you can do with that is tell time."

"Tell time what?" said Woodrow.

"Numbers," said Big John.

"What for?" said Woodrow.

"Don't pester me," said Big John. "You've given me a lump on the head as it is. Go talk to Starboy Mole."

"Who's Starboy Mole?" said Grover.

"I hear he's tunnelling in Poverty Hollow," said Big John and down he went to the bottom of the pond.

A little while later something came through the roof of Starboy's main tunnel and landed with a thump. "That must be some heavy worm!" said Starboy. He hurried to where the hole in the roof was, he looked up with his tiny eyes and waved the twenty-two tentacles on his snout.

"Are you waving hello?" said Grover.

"I'm waving goodbye," said Starboy.

"Are you Starboy Mole?" said Grover.

"Are you waving hello?" said Grover.
"I'm waving goodbye," said Starboy.

"Why should I tell you?" said Starboy. "I don't have any time for nonsense. I've eaten one hundred and seventy-nine worms today and I still have one hundred and twenty-one to go. What's this thing in my tunnel?"

"It's a mystery," said Grover.

"Why didn't you say so to begin with?" said Starboy.

He took hold of the lock with his big hands and turned the knob. "Aha!" he said. He listened to the clicks and he felt the vibrations with his twenty-two tentacles. "Oho!" he said. He turned the knob this way, that way, this way, that way, and *snap!* The lock came open.

"Look at that!" said Woodrow. Starboy closed the lock with his big strong hands. Then he turned the knob this way and that, he listened to the clicks and he felt the vibrations and *snap!* The lock came open again.

"That's really something," said Grover. "What is that thing though?"

"I'll tell you something," said Starboy. "All my life I've pondered why I have great big hands and twenty-two tentacles for a nose."

"And now?" said Grover.

"Ha ha!" said Starboy as he and the combination lock disappeared down the tunnel.

"Well, that's that," said Woodrow.

"Still," said Grover, "it was quite a lot of action while it lasted."

Most of the time Starboy Mole worked very hard right round the clock eating worms.

STARBOY
MOLE

Most of the time Starboy Mole worked very hard right round the clock eating worms. Whenever he could he put some worms aside so he could get a little bit ahead and have some spare time for his combination lock. Sometimes Starboy wondered how in the world he had got along before the lock had come into his life. Grover and Woodrow Crow had dropped it into his tunnel one day and Grover had told him it was a mystery.

"Just like that, a mystery!" Starboy used to say to himself. Who else had a mystery? Nobody that he knew of. Sometimes he would go to special places with it. He would turn the knob and listen to the clicks and feel the vibrations with the twenty-two tentacles on his snout. Starboy had worked out the combination all by himself, just by listening to and feeling the action of the tumblers as he turned the knob. It was a beautiful combination: seventeen clicks left, three right, twelve left, seven right, nine left and *snap!* there it was, open.

Starboy would think about it for a while that way — how it was when it was open. He would hang it on his snout and swing it to and fro, then he would hang it on his left foreleg and dance about a little, then on his right foreleg. "Thus do I dance with an open mystery," he would sing. Then he would close the lock and do the same things with it closed, singing, "Thus do I dance with a closed mystery." He would sit down in silence then and think about the closed-

ness of his mystery. Then all too soon it would be time to go back to his worm work.

Starboy didn't like to be away from his mystery. He began to take it with him when he went worming. He put a hind leg through the shackle and dragged it through his tunnels.

One winter day Starboy was down below the frost line, he was opening up a new branch, he was tunnelling hard. The earth he was moving with his big hands was wet and heavy, it was slow going. Where he was the earth smelled dark and fresh, it smelled of spring but over it the ground was frozen hard.

Starboy smelled other creatures working all round him, worms and millipedes and cicada nymphs. He heard a cicada nymph singing to himself as he worked his way from root to root drinking sap:

"Seventeen years rooting around,
Seventeen years in the cold, cold ground,
One of these days going to find me a summer,
Going to get me a drum and be a hum-tumdrummer."

Starboy began to think of summer and cicadas drumming and the earth moving easy in his hands.

In amongst all the other smells Starboy smelled one special one. It was a speaking smell, it said, "Why don't you come on over here and sit a while?" Starboy had been tunnelling hard but he began to tunnel even harder following that smell. It said different things as he went. It said, "Good friends make the darkness light."

Starboy found that his mystery was slowing him down. He slipped out of it and then he went much faster, he was swimming through the earth like a breast-stroke champion. Starboy's hands were shovelling so fast that he was making a sound like a pumping engine as he surged through the earth-forest of roots and fungus filaments.

Other underground workers said to one

another, "What's that coming down the line like an express train?"

It was Starboy Mole following that special smell that was talking to him in the darkness. It said:

"A little smile, a little song
Make the winter seem less long."

Starboy burst into a tunnel that someone else had already dug. The special speaking smell was very strong in there, and there was a sign that said in Mole:

KOSY KORNER

STELLA VELVET A.S.M.

"Aha!" said Starboy. He knew that A.S.M. meant Association of Star-Nosed Moles.

He came to a charming little door. "This is something like!" said Starboy. He knocked gently.

A beautiful star-nosed mole came to the door. Starboy inhaled her scent.

"Forgive me," he said, "I happened to be passing by when I read your scent and I was so intrigued by it that I couldn't help knocking on your door. I hope that this is not an inconvenient moment?"

"Not at all," said the lady.

"May I introduce myself?" said Starboy.

"I am, Madam, your humble obedient servant, Starboy Mole, A.S.M., B.M.P."

"How do you do," said Stella Velvet. "I'm Stella Velvet, A.S.M. What's B.M.P.?"

"Brotherhood of Mystery Proprietors," said Starboy.

"What kind of mystery?" said Stella.

"Sometimes it's open, sometimes it's closed," said Starboy.

"You're a deep one," said Stella. "Do you like to sing hymns?"

"I don't mind singing hims if I can sing hers once in a while," said Starboy.

"You *are* a devil!" said Stella. "Come and sit beside me while I play the harmolium."

"With pleasure," said Starboy. "What shall we sing?"

"How about *There Is a Warmth Below the Frost Line*?" said Stella.

"That's a good one," said Starboy, and he

"You are *a devil!*" said *Stella*. "*Come and sit
beside me while I play the harmolium.*"

After singing hymns they had tea and little sandwiches. "I've had ever such a pleasant time," said Starboy.

sang with a will while Stella played the harmolium and sang with him. After singing
hymns they had tea and little sandwiches.

"I've had ever such a pleasant time," said
Starboy. "It truly has been delightful
meeting you but I must go now." He was
thinking of his mystery that he had left
far behind him in the winter-dark, fresh,
spring-smelling earth.

"You're thinking of your mystery," said
Stella.

"Yes," said Starboy. "I really can't be
away from it too long, it needs me."

"Ah, well," said Stella. "It *has* been a
pleasant evening. You'll come again?"

"If I may," said Starboy.

Then he went back to his mystery.

"Ah!" he said. "How I've myst you!"

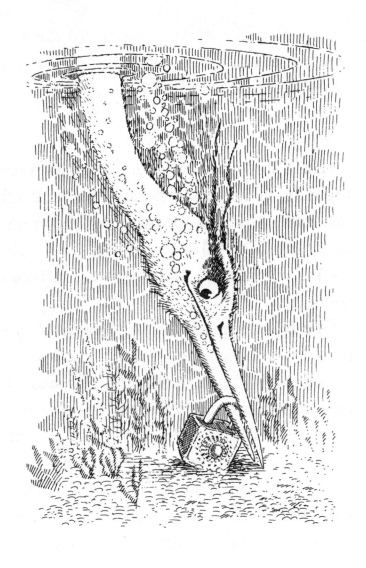

*Joram's beak shot into the water like a
spear thrown hard.*

JORAM
VANDERSTANDER

Joram Vanderstander was a great blue heron. He used to make a joke about it. "I don't say I'm a *great* blue heron," he would say, "but I think I'm a pretty *good* blue heron." Then he would laugh, "Fronk, fronk, fronk."

One foggy spring morning he was standing (or vanderstanding) in the pond like a grey ghost on his high stilt legs. He had his neck in a curve like a flattened S, he made no sound, no move, he was waiting, waiting, watching, watching.

Zzzsss! His beak shot into the water like a spear thrown hard and Joram came up with a rusty combination lock. He knew what it was, he was an experienced old bird. "Well!" he said, "I knew this was a private pond but I never thought they'd start locking up the water. Fronk, fronk, fronk."

He flipped the lock into the lily pads, where it hit a bullfrog. The bullfrog squawked and jumped and Joram caught it and swallowed it down with great gulps. "That's more like it," he said, and flapped away like the ghost of a heron into the fog, his neck like an S, his long legs trailing.

Starboy Mole climbed up onto the bank and shook himself. Joram Vanderstander's beak had just missed him. Starboy looked up into the fog. He could see that it was lighter than the bottom of the pond but he couldn't see any more than that, his eyes weren't much good to him.

"Whoosh!" he said. "Flap, flap, flap, flap."

Joram flapped away like the ghost of a heron into the fog.

*Starboy found the combination lock, hooked a
foot through the shackle, and swam back.*

He lifted his big heavy hands and let them drop again. "Mystery!" he said. "*There's mystery!*"

He slipped into the pond, swam under the lily pads and searched the bottom for the combination lock. He found it, hooked a foot through the shackle, swam back to his underwater tunnel entrance, and crouched in the dark, opening and closing the lock. It had been given to him by Grover and Woodrow Crow, that lock. He had no idea what its proper use might be, it had become his private mystery. All alone he had worked out the combination, it had been his joy and his delight to open it, to close it, to dance with it. Now all at once it seemed nothing at all.

Starboy had of course always known that birds came *down* out of the air but he had never before been near any kind of bird, let alone a great blue heron, when it went *up* into the air. The flapping of Joram's great wings, the suck and gurgle of the water as his long legs went up out of it had suddenly made Starboy feel as if flying was the only thing worth doing.

In the afternoon Joram Vanderstander came flapping slowly back to the pond. He was stalking about in the reeds, lifting his feet and putting them down in perfect silence when he heard a sound from a hole in the bank: "Psst! Psst!"

"Psst who?" said Joram. "Psst what?"

"Psst, Mister Vanderstander," said a little voice, "you like worms?"

"I don't know," said Joram. "It takes so many to make a meal that I don't much bother with them."

"Three hundred and forty-seven worms I've got saved up," said the little voice.

"Really big ones, fresh, nice, very good."

"All right," said Joram, "so you've got three hundred and forty-seven earthworms. What's on your mind?"

"Flying," said the little voice.

"So fly," said Joram.

"No wings," said the little voice.

"Then you're better off not flying," said Joram. "It could be dangerous. Fronk, fronk, fronk."

"I'll give you all my earthworms if you'll take me flying," said the little voice.

"I'm not sure I vanderstand this," said Joram. "Let's have a look at you."

"You'll eat me," said the little voice.

"Well, that'd be one way to go flying with me," said Joram. "Fronk, fronk, fronk, I'm only joking, I won't eat you — this time."

Starboy stuck just his nose out of the hole.

"Are you coming or going?" said Joram. "Fronk, fronk."

"You have your nose, I have mine," said Starboy.

"How about the worms?" said Joram.

"Half now, half when I get back," said Starboy.

"Done," said Joram.

Starboy divided the three hundred and forty-seven worms into two heaps and Joram gulped down one heap. Starboy climbed onto a fallen tree and from there onto Joram's back. Joram spread his wings and up they went into the air.

Starboy could feel all of a sudden that there was nothing under him but Joram. He felt as if he had left his stomach behind. The wind whistled past his nose tentacles and roared in his ears. He closed his tiny eyes and prayed.

Starboy could feel all of a sudden that there was nothing under him but Joram.

"Well," said Joram, "what do you think? Nothing like it, is there?"

"No," said Starboy, gasping for breath.

"Look down," said Joram. "There's Poverty Hollow, there's the pond, there's Frogtown Stump."

Starboy looked down. All he could see was that it was darker under him than it was over him.

"I feel great," said Joram. "Most days I only feel like a good blue heron but today I feel like a great blue heron. Hang on, I'm going to loop the loop."

Up and over went Joram and off came Starboy. Down he plummetted like a black velvet cannonball into the pond. What a splash.

Roland Waters the diving beetle happened to have his head out of the water at the time. He saw Joram loop the loop, he saw Starboy streak out of the sky and into the water, saw him swim back to his tunnel.

"Whoosh!" said Roland. "Sploosh! That's *diving!*"

For the rest of the day he flew up as high as he could and dived into the pond again and again but he hadn't the weight to make a real splash.

*Carrie would hang by her tail for hours
on end but nothing got clearer.*

CARRIE
POSSUM

Carrie Possum was certainly well named. It almost seemed as if when she wasn't carrying six little possums in her pouch she was carrying six fairly large ones on her back. She wasn't bad-looking but she always looked frazzled. Often she didn't know what to do with herself. She would hang by her tail for hours on end but nothing got clearer. Or she would tiptoe down to the road and wait for headlights to cross the road in the glare of.

"Well," she used to say dreamily, "I could have done a whole lot of things but I just don't know anymore." Carrie liked to hang around people's houses. Sometimes she knocked over garbage cans. Once she heard somebody say she was a marsupial and it started a sort of dream in her mind: "Ma Soupial's Kozy Kitchen," she thought. "Ma Soupial's Soulfood Snackery, or maybe Ma Soupial's Pondside Parlour."

She didn't care for dogs at all, oh dear, no. She hated the little ones that yapped, she hated the big ones that roof-roofed as if they owned the world. But most of all she hated and feared one particular hound dog, the one who curdled the night with his HAROO YAROO when he was on a hot trail. He was a big blue-tick hound called Blue, he lived at Todman's Farm on Pilgrim Hill. Pilgrim Hill was the new name, the old name was Gallows Hill, everybody knew that you could smell things there on certain nights, see and hear things too, although nobody would say what.

Nobody that Carrie knew called Blue by his right name, they all called him Old Gallows.

"He don't have no business with us," said Carrie to her friend Purina Rabbit. "A blue-tick hound is a coon hound, everybody knows that."

"Old Gallows don't know it," said Purina. "He might of been bred a coon hound but he ain't never been trained for it. Old Man Todman, he just lets him run loose and he goes after whatever he can get."

"Hear me now," said Carrie to her children, "you mind what Purina says. You keep away from Old Gallows and you keep away from Gallows Hill."

All the same it was Carrie who couldn't keep away from Gallows Hill. She began to have a terrible craving to go there in the dead of night. She began to have dreams in which she heard a little whispery song:

"Thus do I dance with a closed mystery,
Thus do I dance with an open mystery."

"I don't care about no mystery, I don't care if it's open or closed," Carrie said to herself. "For the sake of the children I ain't going nowhere near Gallows Hill."

Week followed week, though, and the children grew up and left home, tiptoeing into the night. One night the full moon was shining right in Carrie's face as if it were putting a question.

"All right," said Carrie. Off she went, heading for Gallows Hill by the light of the moon.

"Thus do I dance with an open mystery,
Thus do I dance with a closed mystery,"

74

sang the voice of her dream. "I don't care about no mystery," said Carrie but she didn't turn back. Carrie could smell the cow pasture and the barn, she could smell what they'd had for supper at Todman's Farm: spaghetti and meatballs. And she could smell Old Gallows, where he'd marked his boundaries that day. Carrie kept on till she came to the lawn in front of the farmhouse. There were a lot of mole tunnels and some of them had been dug up by Old Gallows. She was tiptoeing around when she tiptoed onto something cold and hard and smelling of rust: it was a combination lock. That was when she heard something spooky, she heard a little whispery voice say, "Seventeen left, three right, twelve left, seven right, nine left."

Carrie looked all around and smelt all around but she knew it was a ghost voice

Old Gallows was on her trail and she had to run for it with the lock in her mouth.

she'd heard and she knew it was a ghost smell that she smelled. And she knew what she'd found, she knew a lock when she saw one, she had seen all kinds of sheds and outbuildings smelling of all kinds of good things locked against her.

Carrie had clever hands, she tried the combination and the lock opened. She began to cry. "Here I am with a lock!" she sobbed. "And ary a thing to lock up!"

By then of course Old Gallows was on her trail and she had to run for it with the lock in her mouth. Oh dear, how he chased her all over Gallows Hill, it was unmerciful, Carrie thought her poor heart would burst, what with his HAROO YAROO and the general fright of the thing.

"I'm done!" said Carrie over her shoulder to Old Gallows, "I'm finished, I got nothing left in me, you do whatever you're fixing to do, I don't care no more."

She just let herself go limp, she flopped over in a dead faint with a silly grin on her face and she let out a little sort of dead and gone smell.

Old Gallows almost fell over himself stopping short in the middle of his HAROO YAROO. He'd been thinking to himself, "It won't be but a minute or two and there's going to be some good chomping!" Then all of a sudden there she was in front of him dead to the world with that silly grin and she didn't smell like good chomping at all. "Shoot!" said Old Gallows, "I been wasting my time." He sniffed one more sniff and gave Carrie up as a bad job. He spent the rest of the evening going around marking his boundaries.

When Carrie got home, shaken but safe, she wondered whether she too had been wasting her time. But she had the lock and she found something to lock up. It was down in the dump, a chicken-wire cage one of the Todman boys had made for a crow he'd gotten tired of and let go. Carrie and her friends called it Ma Soupial's Soulfood Snackery. Sometimes when they had something to eat they'd come there and she'd lock the door with the combination lock, then they'd pretend whatever they were eating was cornpone or hominy grits, fatback and collard greens, things like that.

They might hear Old Gallows HAROO YAROOing, they didn't care, he couldn't get into Ma Soupial's Soulfood Snackery.

79

CAVAN COUNTY LIBRARY

THE

END